THE Longest WAIT

WRITTEN BY ALISON BREWIS
ILLUSTRATED BY JENNY BRAKE

Two little children tucked
up in their beds

but they're much too excited
to lay down their heads.

The presents
are wrapped,

the carols are sung,

at the end of the beds,
the stockings are hung.

Tickety tock,
Tickety tock.

It feels like forever,
just watching the clock.

The
Longest
Wait is
nearly
done –

We're
waiting
for
morning
to come.

Mary and Joseph have
packed up their clothes,

with
plenty of
nappies,
and blue
babygros.

The angel said,

"Don't worry,
don't be AFRAID.

This baby is GOD'S

and he's coming to
SAVE!"

Tickety tock,
Tickety tock.

It feels like forever, just watching the clock.

The Longest Wait
is nearly done –

We're waiting for
our baby son.

Anna and Simeon, both very old,
have trusted the promises
God has foretold.

The whole earth is waiting,
it's holding its breath.

When is the end of
sickness and death?

The birds
are a-flutter,
the bees are
a-humming,

the trees start to whisper that

"SOMEONE IS
COMING!"

Tickety tock, Tickety tock.

It feels like forever,
just watching the clock.

The Longest Wait is nearly done –

We're waiting for the victory won!

He's here!
He's here!
It's Christmas
morn!

The Saviour
of the world
is born!

It's such good news,

WooHoo, HooRay!

The king has come,
it's Christmas day!

Tickety tock,
Tickety tock.

It felt like forever, just watching the c

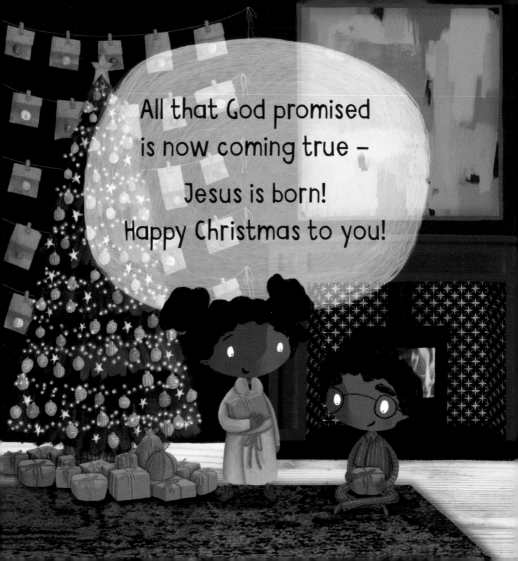

All that God promised
is now coming true –

Jesus is born!
Happy Christmas to you!

A free download for
extended play is available
at 10ofThose.com

For Nicholas, Ana and Isabelle

The Longest Wait
Text and Illustrations © 2019 Alison Brewis and Jenny Brake.

Published by 10Publishing, a division of 10ofThose Limited.
ISBN 978-1-912373-93-2

Typeset by Diane Warnes.

10ofThose Limited, Unit C Tomlinson Road, Leyland, PR25 2DY
Email: info@10ofthose.com   Website: www.10ofthose.com